SPECIALS

stewpot

TALES FROM A FANTASY TAVERN

A tavern simulation roleplaying game for 3+ players

by Takuma Okada

An Evil Hat Productions publication

www.evilhat.com • feedback@evilhat.com
@EvilHatOfficial • facebook.com/EvilHatProductions

Stewpot: Tales From a Fantasy Tavern

EHP0068 • ISBN 978-1-61317-211-7

First published in 2024 by Evil Hat Productions, LLC,
10125 Colesville Rd #318, Silver Spring, MD 20901.

Printed in the United States of America.

EVIL HAT PRODUCTIONS

stewpot

TALES FROM A FANTASY TAVERN

CREDITS

AUTHOR/DEVELOPER/DESIGNER
Takuma Okada

EDITOR
Jacky Leung

COVER ARTIST
Elemei

ART DIRECTOR
Lucia Seersword

PROOFREADER
Jenn Martin

SENSITIVITY READER
Basil Wright

RECIPES
Krista D. Ball

SYSTEM DEVELOPMENT CONSULTANTS
Meguey Baker and D. Vincent Baker

INTERIOR ARTISTS
Arthur Cabezas, Elemei, Franz Michael A. Bautista, Gryme, Jasprismatic, Kelsey Phillips, Linden Medina, Lorne Colt, Rhie Cueva, Xylica

PLAYTESTERS
Aaron Lim, adam mcconnaughey, Bae "forever DM" jiho, crtgirl, Daffodil, Drew Owen, Dylan Silcox, Eames Maxwell, Harm ten Napel, Johanna Gaudet, Kris Allison, Lorenzo Occhialini, Marc Majcher, Margot Mutter, Marley Hannan, Matthias N, Michael D., Michael Pureka, Mya Shishido, NPC-san, Rayven Reid-Murray, Richard Todd, Sean Hayes, Simone Di Rubbo, Trystan Goetze, Vivian, Weston L. Marigold Humphreys, WhatNames, Woolstone

LAYOUT & GRAPHIC DESIGN
Cris Viana

VTT DEVELOPER
Sophie Lagacé

MARKETING MANAGER
Tom Lommel

BUSINESS DEVELOPMENT
Chris Hanrahan

PROJECT MANAGER
Sean Nittner

PRODUCT DEVELOPER
Fred Hicks

CREDIT FOR DERIVATIVE WORK
Based on The Sundered Land, Psi*run/Otherkind Dice and the Firebrands Framework by Meguey Baker and D. Vincent Baker

stewpot

TALES FROM A FANTASY TAVERN

Introduction

It was a few years after I left home. I was broke. I didn't have a steady party, and I was failing most of my quests. I walked into this place that looked real run down, figuring it was cheap.

I remember the moment I walked in, how warm it felt in there. There was a crackling fire with a huge pot hanging over it. I ordered soup because that was all I could afford, and the biggest bowl I had ever seen in my life was set down in front of me with a whole loaf of bread, too.

I was halfway through the meal and flagging when one of the tavern keepers came and sat across from me. I got nervous, thinking there'd been a mistake. When that didn't seem to be the case, I started feeling embarrassed that I wouldn't be able to finish the food. It was a relief when she started tearing off pieces of bread and dipping them in the soup.

It was the first meal I'd eaten in a long time where I didn't feel so alone.

You know the feeling all too well. Stumbling through a thick forest, living off stale rations, unable to get a full night's sleep. When you finally arrive at the next town, the tavern is where you find all the comforts of civilization that you've sorely missed.

Your party has been adventuring for many years now. It's a tough job, and it only gets tougher as time goes on. Many adventurers end their travels early. While some prefer a quiet retirement, others remain as restless as they were during their prime. It's quite common for former adventurers to keep busy by running taverns, where they offer shelter, food, and advice to the younger generation. That's what you've decided to do. Together.

Stewpot: Tales from a Fantasy Tavern is a collection of mini-games that tell the story of a tavern run by former adventurers. It's about hanging up your weapons, selling off your armor, and integrating back into society.

Materials

- Tavern and character sheets (or blank paper)
- Writing utensils
- One or more six-sided dice (ideally, at least six)
- A deck of cards
- A coin

Download Character and Tavern sheets at ***www.evilhat.com***

Safety: Breaks and Holds

Stewpot utilizes two safety tools built into the game, in addition to any you may wish to use. Even in a lighthearted game like *Stewpot*, it's important to have them available. Player safety is more important than any idea you bring up in a game.

Taking a Break

After playing three mini-games, take a break before you start ***Wear and Tear***. Optionally, you can also call for a break after finishing any mini-game if anyone needs one.

During a break, take five or more minutes to clear your head. Everyone should step away from the play area or table. If you're playing online: get up, stretch, or walk around for a bit. Grab food and water. Avoid thinking about the game while on break.

After the break, players may ask each other about any changes to the story so far, or discuss story elements they would like to work toward in later mini-games.

Holds

Anyone can call for a HOLD at any time. Your group should agree on what gesture calls for a Hold before starting the game. A gesture could be:

- Holding up a hand or fist
- Placing a hand or fist in the middle of the table
- Sending a message that says "HOLD" in your group chat for an online game
- Saying HOLD out loud
- Reacting to a message with an emoji that your group has designated as a hold symbol

When a player calls for a Hold, all play should stop. When everyone at the table is ready, discuss what happened and work towards a solution. The person who initiated the Hold should speak first. Players may take a break before starting this conversation.

Don't be afraid to change or retcon anything that needs it. If anyone is no longer comfortable playing the game for now, the game is over. There's always another time. Your fellow players come first.

Your Tavern

"Why are you always sketching in that journal?"

"It's inspiration. I wouldn't expect you to get it."

"Rude. For what? That's a table."

"Yeah, and it's really sturdy, and the color of the stain is nice and calming, and it's octagonal but the corners are rounded off so no one gets hurt when they get thrown into it. Well. Not hurt badly, at least. Hopefully."

"You're still set on that tavern thing, huh?"

"You said you'd help!"

"I did. I will! Promise."

Your tavern and the area around it are the cornerstones of your game. Your adventurers will be living and working here, and they'll take time off and join festivals and other events in town. Work together to create a place you're excited to play in.

Location

Do you want to compete with other taverns in a bustling city, or do you want to be a little stop in the wilderness, the only place to stay in a small town?

As a group, decide the size and scale of your town or city. Then, each player provides one detail about the city or surrounding area.

EXAMPLES (CITY):

- Canals instead of streets
- Connected treehouses
- Floating, in water or air
- Ancient and crumbling
- Carved into a cliff
- Criss-crossing bridges over deep canyons
- Beautiful stained glass windows
- Old brick buildings
- Giant murals
- Flowers covering the walls of buildings

EXAMPLES (ENVIRONMENT):

- Deserts littered with enormous bones
- Underground tunnels illuminated by glowing stones
- Low sloping mountains
- Humid
- Snowbanks and frozen lakes
- Towering trees
- Megafauna
- A coastline of floating rock

Look

What does your tavern look like? Be as general or as specific as you like. What interests you the most about a building? What draws your eye?

EXAMPLES:

- Dark gray stone blocks
- Reclaimed materials
- Mossy walls
- Flowering vines
- Delicately carved sandstone
- Ice palace
- Boat
- Wrought iron
- A unique weathervane

Name

Don't spend too long on this one! Feel free to come back to it if you're stuck, and remember you can always change it if you come up with a new name during play.

You can also come up with a symbol or emblem to go with the name. A chipped-paint sign outside really completes the look.

EXAMPLES:

- The Old Bell Tavern
- The Rose Without Thorns
- The Greasy Snifter
- The Boar Hat
- Fortune's Rest
- Fairweather's

Tavern Ratings

Your tavern becomes larger and more well-known as you improve its TAVERN RATINGS. These ratings determine the quality of different aspects of your tavern, as well as the dice you roll in certain games. You start with **one point** in each rating.

Cuisine

Your CUISINE RATING determines your tavern's ability to make food. It includes your skill at cooking food, food storage, relationships with suppliers, and more.

1 — *A cramped kitchen. Plenty of staples but nothing fancy.*

2 — *A modest kitchen. New friends at the market.*

3 — *A bustling kitchen. Brand new cookware. A well-stocked spice cabinet.*

4 — *A splendid kitchen. Good deals on ingredients and fresh deliveries. Specialized tools.*

Atmosphere

Your ATMOSPHERE RATING determines the experience patrons have at your tavern. The smells, the decorations, and the chatter of folks eating at tables around you are all part of the atmosphere. The higher your rating gets, the more comfortable the tavern becomes. A higher rating may also mean offering unique experiences not found at other taverns.

1 — *Comfortable enough, but a little boring. Things feel slightly off.*

2 — *A little plain, but homey. Not a bad place to get a good night's sleep.*

3 — *Furniture and decorations that highlight the area. Lots of personal touches. It's really starting to come together.*

4 — *The comfiest beds you've ever slept in. Lots of light and good company. Adventurers seek you out after long journeys.*

Service

Your SERVICE RATING is a measure of how well your tavern operates. Is the food getting out quickly and to the right tables? Are the beds clean and comfy? Your service rating also determines the caliber and amount of people you can afford to hire.

Every time you gain a point in your SERVICE RATING, you create a new NPC employee as one of the many new hires. Come up with one or use one of the examples listed.

1 — *A former farmhand, an injured local guard.*

2 — *An experienced line cook, good wait staff.*

3 — *An interior decorator, a skilled executive chef.*

4 — *An accomplished head of staff, a prestigious sommelier.*

Tavern Advancement

Your tavern starts off small and kind of shabby. But with hard work and more than a little luck, you hope to become a home away from home for all adventurers passing through.

As you play mini-games, time passes. Your characters become better at running the tavern, and word spreads.

After every third mini-game, take a break to check in. Then play ***Wear and Tear*** to increase one of your Tavern Ratings by one, up to a maximum of four.

You can also choose to play ***Wear and Tear*** on your turn to increase a Tavern Rating by one. This resets the timer to play ***Wear and Tear*** every three mini-games.

You can also increase a Tavern Rating instantly by succeeding in the ***Festival Day*** or ***A Distinguished Guest*** mini-games. This does not reset the timer to play ***Wear and Tear***. If you play ***Homegrown***, your Cuisine Rating gains a bonus point during your next playthrough of ***Wear and Tear***.

Each time a Tavern Rating increases, each player may describe a new detail or feature for the tavern.

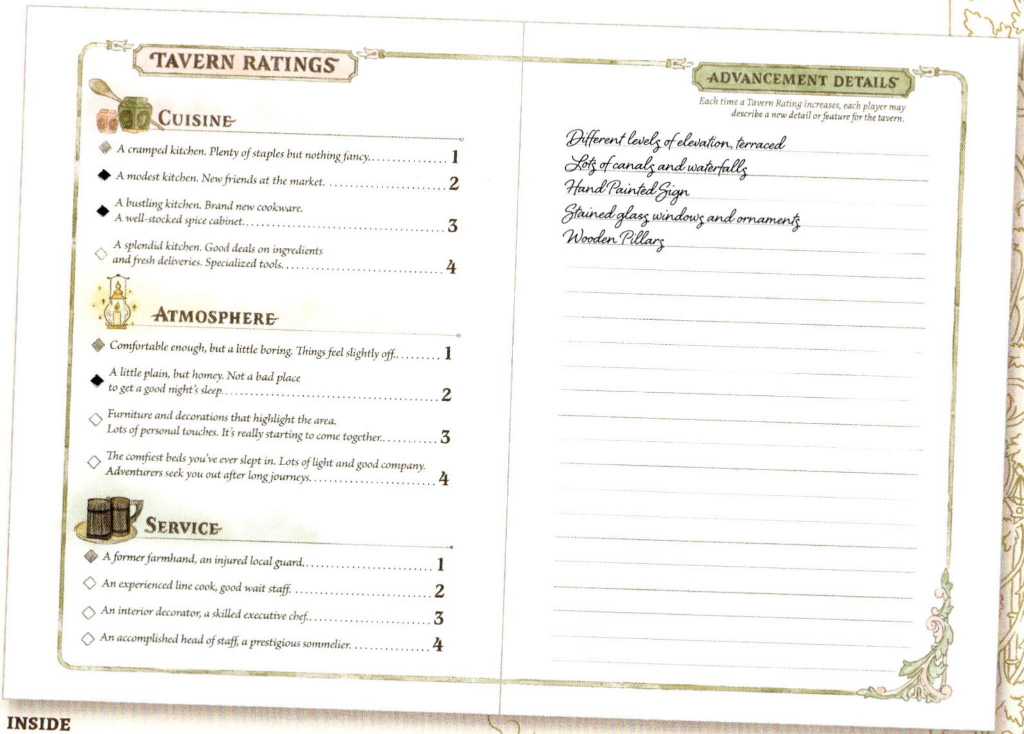

TAVERN RATINGS

CUISINE

- A cramped kitchen. Plenty of staples but nothing fancy. 1
- A modest kitchen. New friends at the market. 2
- A bustling kitchen. Brand new cookware. A well-stocked spice cabinet. 3
- A splendid kitchen. Good deals on ingredients and fresh deliveries. Specialized tools. 4

ATMOSPHERE

- Comfortable enough, but a little boring. Things feel slightly off. 1
- A little plain, but homey. Not a bad place to get a good night's sleep. 2
- Furniture and decorations that highlight the area. Lots of personal touches. It's really starting to come together. 3
- The comfiest beds you've ever slept in. Lots of light and good company. Adventurers seek you out after long journeys. 4

SERVICE

- A former farmhand, an injured local guard. 1
- An experienced line cook, good wait staff. 2
- An interior decorator, a skilled executive chef. 3
- An accomplished head of staff, a prestigious sommelier. 4

ADVANCEMENT DETAILS

Each time a Tavern Rating increases, each player may describe a new detail or feature for the tavern.

Different levels of elevation, terraced
Lots of canals and waterfalls
Hand Painted Sign
Stained glass windows and ornaments
Wooden Pillars

INSIDE

Pastries

Creating your Characters

Autumn leaves and rusted blade

Dented shields and flickering flame

Warrior, what is your fate?

Tattered robes and crumbling stone

Ragged breath and broken bow

Warrior, where will you go?

Aching scars and restless nights,

The cold inside your bones.

Hands so skilled at taking life,

Must learn to help it grow.

Your characters are the heart of your tavern. You keep the kitchen running, the fires roaring, the beds made, and the tables clean. To make your character, you need a few key things:

- A name
- A look (Weapon, Armor, and Quirk)
- An Adventurer Job
- Three Adventurer Experiences
- A Town Job

As you play, you'll also write down KEEPSAKES.

Name

Your character's name can be given, chosen, or something else. In addition to your character's true name, some characters might have a nickname that their coworkers and regulars use instead.

Look

Your character can look like anything, but their clothes, the things they carry, and how they move through the world reveals their past. What parts of being an adventurer still show? What have they worked to change?

Come up with your own details or choose one Weapon, Armor, and Quirk from the table.

WEAPON	ARMOR	QUIRK
A giant sword, all blunt edges and fierce	*A rusty suit of armor with a deadly curse*	*Eyes always watching*
A staff of dark wood, worn smooth	*An iridescent cloak of feathers*	*One hand hidden under a cloak*
A sturdy shield polished to a shine	*Concealed leather and chainmail*	*Hair cut short with a knife*
Twin jeweled daggers	*Black boots with not a speck of dust on them*	*Slow, measured movements*
A bow that seems to hum when drawn	*Gloves covered in runes*	*A smile that doesn't reach your eyes*
Spiked gauntlets covered in dents	*Clothes the color of deep forest*	*Shoulders that tense to the sound of metal*
A crossbow covered in unknown mechanisms	*A mask*	*A preference for sitting in dark corners*
A simple sabre	*A well kept traveling cloak*	*Sleeping with one eye open*
A dirk with a curious carved hilt	*A warm coat*	*Perfectly straight posture*
An enormous hammer carved from bone	*Armor crafted from a giant insect shell*	*Always muttering wards of protection*
A sword that whispers in its scabbard	*A tattered royal tunic*	*A gleaming smile*

Jobs and Experiences

When you create your character, pick an Adventurer Job and a Town Job. Pick three ADVENTURER EXPERIENCES, but no TOWN EXPERIENCES yet. Characters can have the same jobs or experiences. If some of the experiences in a job don't make sense for your character, create your own appropriate experiences or borrow from other jobs.

Your jobs represent roles or activities you took on as an adventurer, and what you do now in town. They're a bit like classes or playbooks you might find in other games. Your experiences are special skills, training, feats, knowledge, etc., you've accumulated from your time as an adventurer or living in town.

As you play mini-games, you'll use your experiences to overcome obstacles. When you use an Adventurer Experience, cross it out. At the end of that mini-game, you'll gain a Town Experience in exchange.

When an experience is crossed out, it doesn't disappear. It served you well at one point. It might be hard to see yourself as someone that doesn't do that anymore. But you don't need it here. You can put it away for now.

Briefly describe how you let go of that Adventurer Experience and how your time in town helps you gain this Town Experience.

List of Jobs and Experiences

ADVENTURER JOBS

- Paladin
- Wizard
- Fighter
- Rogue
- Druid
- Bard
- Ranger
- Swashbuckler

TOWN JOBS

- Farmer
- Healer
- Chef
- Poet
- Merchant
- Crafter
- Scholar
- Lookout
- Apothecary
- Hunter

Adventurer Jobs and Experiences

PALADIN	
Guidance	*A sign from your deity*
Holy Armor	*Divine protection*
Healing Touch	*Treat wounds*
Smite	*Destroy the unholy*
Taunt	*Draw enemies towards you*

WIZARD	
Prestidigitation	*Small wonders*
Fireball	*Mastery of flame*
Invisibility	*Move unseen*
Magic Missile	*Projectiles of astounding accuracy*
Arcana	*Vast knowledge of the magical and unusual*

FIGHTER	
Intimidation	*Make them do what you want*
Master of Arms	*Armed and dangerous with anything*
Brute Strength	*Move the immovable*
Endurance	*Nothing can stop you*
Legendary Weapon	*An artifact of immense power*

ROGUE	
Cat's Grace	*Extraordinary agility*
Nimble Fingers	*No lock stays locked, no trap can catch you*
Lightfoot	*Act undetected*
Adder's Fangs	*Deadly poisons and their antidotes*
Sixth Sense	*Never be caught off guard*

DRUID	
Green Thumb	*An affinity for plant magic*
Natural Armor	*Skin becomes bark or stone*
Shapeshifter	*Various animal forms*
Naturespeak	*Understand plants and animals*
Force of Nature	*Bend the land around you to your will*

BARD	
Bag of Tricks	*Card magic, juggling clubs, and other spectacles*
Devil's Fingers	*Prodigious skill with an instrument*
Alluring Voice	*The voice of an angel*
Golden Words	*Convince anyone of anything*
Inspiration	*Power up your friends*

RANGER	
Deadeye	*Pinpoint accuracy*
True North	*Unerring sense of direction*
Animal Companion	*A wild friend*
Tracking	*Follow any trail*
Camouflage	*Disappear into nature*

SWASHBUCKER	
Duellist	*Master of the blade*
In the Rigging	*Climbing and acrobatic feats*
Sea Legs	*Balance on any surface*
Barbed Tongue	*Your words hit where they hurt*
Bravado	*Never falter*

Town Jobs and Experiences

FARMER

Preservation	*Make food taste better and last longer*
Weathervane	*Predict the weather a few days in advance*
Bounty	*Your harvests are large and exquisite*
Handler	*Caring for and communicating with animals*
Home Remedies	*Unconventional solutions*

HEALER	
Warm Presence	*You are comforting to be around*
Safe Haven	*Know how to make a space feel welcoming*
Thanatologist	*Help the dead find peace, help the living grieve*
Ritual	*Know the traditions and customs of many*
Bandage Wounds	*Treat injuries*

CHEF	
Clean Cut	*Mince, dice, chop, slice*
Grillmaster	*Expert at grilling food and subordinates*
Parts Unknown	*Knowledge of ingredients from all over*
Refined Palate	*A sense of taste second to none*
Call the Shots	*Quick thinking and split-second decisions*

POET	
Spin Straw into Gold	*Tell enchanting stories*
Say the Right Thing	*Tell them what they want or need to hear*
Chronicler	*Make sure people will remember*
Parable	*A lesson for every situation*
A Friend in Need	*Know who to call for a favor*

MERCHANT	
Trader	*Something I need for something you need*
Network	*Able to obtain anything*
The Back Room	*Satisfy most everyday needs*
The Perfect Gift	*Know exactly what people want*
Well-Traveled	*Know the customs and languages of the world*

CRAFTER	
Finesse	*Acute manual dexterity*
Repair	*Fix anything, with enough time*
Artisan	*Create beautiful things*
Mason	*Build strong structures*
Patron	*You have a wealthy benefactor*

SCHOLAR	
Well Read	*You know it, or you know where to learn it*
Jury Rigging	*Invent your way out of a sticky situation*
Keen Observation	*Something only you could see*
Defuse	*Handle something dangerous*
Streamline	*Get it done faster*

LOOKOUT	
Eyes on the Horizon	*Spot trouble before it starts*
Ears on the Ground	*You heard it first*
Organizer	*Bring people together*
Garrison	*You never have to work alone*
Shoulder Throw	*Defend yourself when necessary*

APOTHECARY	
Brewer	*Concoct potions, salves, balms, and more*
Smell the Flowers	*A keen nose, mastery of scents*
Pipeleaf	*Calm the nerves*
Botanist	*Know every plant in the area*
Distillation	*Strengthen the good in something*

HUNTER	
The Usual Spot	*Know the best areas for hunting and foraging*
Trapper	*A steady supply of meat and furs*
Secret Paths	*Know the area like the back of your hand*
Lying in Wait	*Master of concealment*
Offerings	*On good terms with the local spirits*

Keepsakes

KEEPSAKES are items, trinkets, ephemera, and other physical reminders of the relationships between your characters. They can be a wide range of things: tickets to a show, a funky little clay guy you found at the market, a necklace made out of a shard of an old weapon, a cookbook you hunted down that you think your friend would really like, a dried flower, a basket that you pass back and forth filled with baked goods, or a wooden spoon you carved.

Some of the mini-games mention Keepsakes directly, usually at the end. Most of them don't, and a few are indirect. If something comes up in a game and it feels right, write it down.

CHARACTER SHEET

NAME: Nara they/she pronouns

LOOK: Spiky hair, always wearing a smirk on their face

WEAPON	Rusty spear
ARMOR	Embroidered leather armor
QUIRK	Darting eyes

ADVENTURER JOB	ADVENTURER EXPERIENCES
Wizard	Nimble Fingers - No lock stays locked, no trap can catch you
	Fireball - Mastery of flame
	Magic Missile - Projectiles of astounding accuracy

TOWN JOB	TOWN EXPERIENCES
Hunter	The Usual Spot - Know the best areas for hunting and foraging
	Secret Paths - Know the surrounding area like the back of your hand
	Lying in Wait - Master of concealment
	Offerings - On good terms with the local spirits

KEEPSAKES

- Pat happened. (hiding a bit from them with Will)
- Buttercup taking notes on the dish

stewpot

Playing the Game

When the bowl was finally empty, the tavern keeper told me she was an old adventurer. She had endless stories. I told her I was mostly on my own right now, and she told me it took five or six years to find her party. They were inseparable for twenty years, and when they finally settled down, they started the tavern together. One of them left to travel, and one of them passed a few years back. But the other two came over in between helping guests and shared their own stories.

We talked until the tavern was empty. She looked at the wear on the grip of my sword and said I had been holding my index fingers too tight. She even scolded me for not sharpening and oiling the blade enough. When I admitted I didn't have a place to stay that night, she let me sleep at the tavern, bedroll spread out in front of the hearth.

As I got ready to leave the next morning, I noticed the busted rivet on my armor had been fixed. There was a bag full of rations in my pack too: catoblepas cheese, giant scorpion jerky, a few beautiful apples, and a sticky little pouch of candied chestnuts.

It's hard to say if that night was the reason I kept adventuring. Maybe it wasn't. But I always remembered how she helped me.

Once you've created your tavern and characters, everyone starts with *The First Step* mini-game. Then, take turns choosing other mini-games to play. Invite other players often, and come up with your own prompts or scenes if the listed examples don't feel quite right.

After completing a mini-game, write down any Keepsakes and check if anyone wants to take a break. Otherwise, the next player chooses a mini-game.

Every three mini-games, take a break. When you return, play ***Wear and Tear*** and upgrade the tavern.

The First Step and ***In the Rhythm of Things*** mini-games are only played as the first and last mini-games and cannot be chosen on your turn.

Ending the Game

When every player has exchanged all of their Adventurer Experiences for Town Experiences, play the ***In the Rhythm of Things*** mini-game to conclude the story of your tavern.

After the hard work of getting your tavern up and running, your adventurers could probably use some rest. All games come to an end, and hopefully, you can walk away from *Stewpot* knowing your adventurers have settled down comfortably.

Mini-Games

"You need to eat."

"I'm not hungry."

"I thought the whole point of opening this place was a good meal and a full night's sleep. And I know the second part of that isn't happening tonight. So..."

"Alright, alright. Fine."

It was hard to get that stew down. Nothing to do with Aina's cooking. I was just too nervous. We had to sit on the front steps so I would stop fretting about every little detail inside.

We stayed like that for a while. Watched the sun go down. Lanterns were lit, then blown out, and we saw the stars so clearly that night. At some point, I finally nodded off with my head on Aina's shoulder.

"Hey. It's time, sleepyhead."

"Ugh. God. I'm so sore. Why did we do this?"

"Because I'm an anxious mess, and you're a huge softie. Come on. Let's get some breakfast."

And we've been here ever since.

This is a reference for all of the mini-games that make up *Stewpot*, with a short summary for each one. Each mini-game also has suit symbols next to the title that indicates the type of gameplay involved.

Games that are good intro picks after *The First Step*.

Games with core mechanics or a unique structure.

Games that are mainly prompts for freeform roleplay.

Games that let you upgrade the tavern.

What were you doing before you decided to put down roots here? What was the first thing you learned about how to live in town?

Your adventuring days may be over, but there are plenty of people in town that could use your help.

A Friendly Tavern Brawl 92

Every tavern has its rowdy patrons. They're good at heart, but sometimes when the ale is flowing and spirits are high, things get out of hand.

Festival Day 96

Your town has a few festival days a year, and they're some of your busiest. How do you prepare?

Retracing 102

Adventuring never left you much free time. Starting the tavern was exhausting, but it's the slow season now. You could close up for a while if you wanted.

A Bard's Tale 106

During your time as an adventurer, you accomplished many daring deeds. In fact, some of those deeds are retold to this day by traveling bards.

Sometimes a troubled adventurer comes in looking for answers at the bottom of a glass. Can you help them with more than just a drink?

Someone important is in town and they're almost here. The tavern has to be at its best for this guest. After all, they might leave a generous tip.

As an adventurer, you said farewell many times. Sometimes it was only temporary. Most of the time, it wasn't.

Time passes. Rough edges are sanded down. Before you know it, life in town has become like breathing.

The First Step

What were you doing before you decided to stay in this town? What was the first thing you learned about life after adventuring?

Setup

Everyone plays. Every character gains one Town Experience. Take turns describing a short scene that led to that experience. Other characters can be in your scene, but they won't gain the same experience.

Example Scenes

- A townsperson you helped once welcomes you back. They become your mentor, of sorts, passing on their skills.
- You find a good spot in town to sit and observe. Day by day, you learn what it's like to live here.
- You told yourself long ago that you'd go fishing once you were settled. A friend takes you to a quiet riverbank just outside town.
- A merchant offers you a good price for some of your adventuring gear.
- The children in the town take a liking to you. They pester you for more stories.
- An early frost threatens to kill several fields of crops and the whole town is roused before dawn to help save them. It's a lot more difficult than you thought.

- You befriend the local stray cats. Feeding them becomes part of your morning routine.
- The seeds you planted in a little box by the window have finally started to sprout.
- You've been practicing your cooking and finally feel confident enough to invite some friends over for dinner.
- At first, you were just a patron, but you've somehow found yourself helping out at the local library or literary salon.
- You've been doing some crafts as a hobby (woodworking, embroidery, knitting, weaving, pottery, etc.) and you're presenting a friend with something you've made for the first time.
- You've been sharing all the tips and tricks you picked up taking care of injuries on the road with people in the town.

NPC Sidequest

Your adventuring days may be over, but there are plenty of people in town that could use your help.

Setup

Anyone can play. Decide where you are when you encounter this sidequest. Are you in the tavern? Walking around town? On the road leading in? Other players can jump in, ask questions, add details, or play NPCs throughout the mini-game.

The Quest

NPC Sidequest has three scenes. If you already have a quest in mind, go straight to the scenes. You can also create a quest using the *Creating a Quest* instructions.

The three scenes are:

THE INITIAL REQUEST: What are they asking you to do? What is the situation?

UNDERTAKING THE QUEST: What are the obstacles along the way? You can ask other players for suggestions. How do you accomplish your task?

THE RETURN AND REWARD: Do you come back exhausted? Triumphant? Irritated? What did they promise to give you in exchange for your help?

Creating a Quest

You will need a **standard deck of playing cards** and a **six-sided die** to create a quest. Draw a card from the deck and roll the die. The card drawn determines what kind of quest your character is on and who gave it to you. The die roll determines any complications that may occur.

The Card

DIAMONDS: Diamonds are delivery quests. Someone needs you to pick up or drop something off, sometimes multiple somethings. Maybe it's across town, but they're too busy to get it themselves. Maybe it's a three-day trip to the next town for a precious item.

CLUBS: Clubs are gathering quests. Herbs for the apothecary, spices for the kitchen, minerals for new paint, etc. Towns and taverns both need large amounts of gatherable resources.

HEARTS: Hearts are quests for dealing with pests. Giant rat infestations, mosquitoes, flocks of noisy geese, etc. They usually aren't anywhere near as dangerous as what you used to deal with as an adventurer, but they're somehow just as annoying.

SPADES: Spades are crafting quests. It could be pretty much anything from furniture, special potions, fine clothes, construction tools, or fences. These towns often lack quite a few craftspeople, so a lot of people come to you.

A: A local official

2: A captain of the guard

3: A farmer on the edge of town

4: A burly baker

5: A veteran courier

6: A precocious child

7: A young parent

8: A kind teacher

9: An apprentice carpenter

10: A traveling merchant

J: A trusted regular

Q: A deity or spirit

K: A noble

The Die

1-2: This is going to take a while. You'll need someone to cover your shift at the tavern.

3-4: You need some of your old adventuring gear to do this and it's been buried under other things in your room.

5-6: This is exactly like that other time. When did you last do a quest like this?

Wear and Tear

There's always something to fix, clean, or pay off.

Setup

Anyone can play. As a group, decide what parts of the tavern need fixing and touching up, and what you're adding to the tavern. After playing this mini-game, you may increase one of your TAVERN RATINGS by one.

Working Together

Each player character describes what they're working on.

- Ask another player character for help. Describe how you combine one of your experiences with one of theirs to great effect.
- As you're working, you observe a townsperson or another player character. Describe what you learn from your observation.
- You're completely in your element. Describe how you use an experience to get the work done lightning fast.
- You come up with the perfect food or drink to give everyone some energy. What is it and what's the secret ingredient?
- You notice everyone flagging through a frustrating stretch of work. How do you lift everyone's spirits?
- Everyone loves your idea for a new addition to the tavern. They put you in charge, but you're doubting your own ability to lead. Who gives you encouragement and how?

- What part of the renovation requires everyone to pitch in all at once?
- You're struggling to make progress, but you know exactly which townsperson to ask for help. How did you know they would be good at this?
- It's time for a break and you think it would do everyone a world of good if they let off a little steam. What activity (cards, sparring, a ball game, a race, a funny face battle, etc.) do you suggest everyone participate in and how does it go?
- There was an accident and someone was hurt. Fortunately, it wasn't life-threatening, but they definitely need to be patched up. Who helps them?
- You tell everyone you'll treat them to food after the work is done at a well-loved spot in town. What is this place called? What is everyone planning on ordering?

A Fleeting Moment

Something about the way the fire flickers lingers in your mind. The smell of hay and clover brings a tear to your eye. A fading memory resurfaces. What do you still carry from your old life?

Setup

One character remembers. The character's player finds an object in their pockets, on the table, or around the room.

Other players can add details or ask questions during the game.

Reminiscing

Examine the object. Touch or turn it in your hands if you can. Smell or taste it if you can. What memory does this bring up?

EXAMPLE MEMORIES

- A meager meal out on the road
- The morning before a desperate battle
- Getting up to mischief
- A sunrise like no other
- An unsolved puzzle
- A mysterious being
- You took a blow for me
- Carvings among the ruins
- The scent of a certain flower
- An ill-fated romance
- Antics, recklessness, old friends
- Pursuing an old grudge
- A request from a ghost
- It was during a downpour
- We had gotten separated from the rest of the group

In Time

When you are done describing the memory, choose one.

HOLD ON: You don't want to lose this one. Keep the object near you for the rest of the game.

LET GO: Let the memory fade. Change one of your Adventurer Experiences to a Town Experience.

Shields and Skillets

Enchantments are volatile things, especially when they sit unused for years. A long time ago, many retired adventurers died in tragic accidents caused by their old enchanted equipment. Homes were leveled, sometimes even whole towns. Many believed these disasters were caused by the curses an adventurer accumulated over their career.

Certain enchanters eventually realized the root of the problem, but they couldn't separate the magical and physical on their own. It takes a high level of skill in both disciplines to disentangle the work that created such an item. This is why enchanters and blacksmiths often travel in pairs. One such pair has just arrived now.

Setup

Everyone plays. Take turns describing items and telling stories about them. First, the owner of an enchanted item describes it. Then, any other character in the group can tell a story of how the item was used in the past. Tell at least one story for each item.

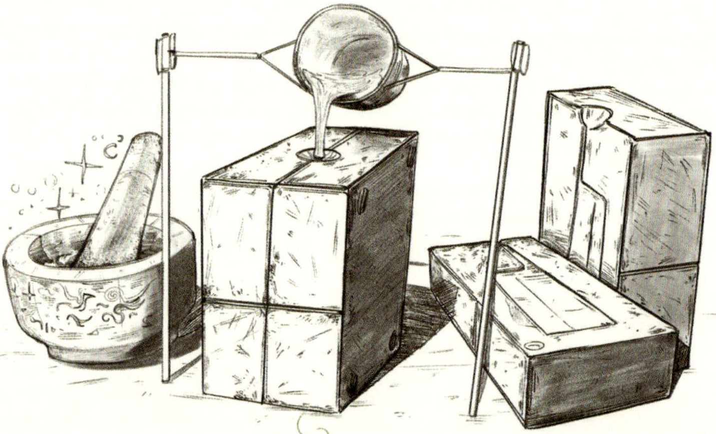

Stories from the Past

- The time you saved my life
- A desperate defense
- Back to back in the middle of a fierce battle
- An unexpected solution to a puzzle
- A breaking point, a reforging
- A glorious duel
- A daredevil feat
- An absurd situation

Letting Go

The enchanter and the blacksmith are ready. Once everyone has told their stories, the item's owner tells the group how they got it in the first place.

For each weapon, flip a coin.

HEADS: The item is safely disenchanted. The blacksmith asks if you would like to forge it into something new.

TAILS: Disaster is narrowly averted. There is very little of the item left to salvage. How do you say goodbye?

You may give someone a Keepsake made from the remnants of your enchanted item.

Market Day

You never would have guessed how many things a tavern needs to operate on a day-to-day basis. It feels like you're always at the market. In your previous life, you would have just thrown your coin at the nearest merchant to get what you needed.

But now that you're tied down to one place, it's not as easy to get everything. Buying something isn't as straightforward as a simple transaction.

Still, calling this place home has its advantages. A trader saves something special for you, or throws in a little something extra as thanks for your patronage, or for that favor you did them last time. It's nice.

Setup

Anyone can play. You will need at least two players. Choose between being a SHOPPER or a MERCHANT.

SHOPPERS: What do you need for the tavern or for yourself? Is it difficult to find here, and if so, why?

MERCHANTS: What sign, item of clothing, or other visual cue do you use to attract buyers?

The Exchange

For each item a Shopper needs, a Merchant can ask a question or ask for help. They may ask as many times as they want until they are satisfied.

- Something hard to find demands something equally rare in return. What piece of valuable adventuring gear can you trade me?
- I don't need the money at the moment, but I need something done that I can't quite handle on my own. Could you, as a former adventurer, handle it?
- I traveled a long way to obtain this, and I have a story to tell. Will you listen to me tell it? Have you been there before too?
- You're told to wait the rest of the day for a shipment to be prepared. As you're wandering the market, you spot a tiny stall that seems to call to you. What do you find inside?
- You once told me a story about your home, and I could see you missed it dearly. I have a little something from there to give you, as a gift for being a regular. What is it?
- I've got this strange object that another trader was getting rid of, and I'm not quite sure what it does. Is it rare or dangerous? Who might want it?
- I'm driving a hard bargain, but I'm the only one selling this thing you desperately need. You've heard I'm in a tough spot. Can you find a way to help me and get what you need?
- You know what foods I like, and how to prepare them. I always give you a discount when you bring me something you've cooked. What have you brought today?

- We've been doing business for a while now, ever since you first settled down here. What do I notice about you that's changed since that first meeting?
- Who do we realize we both know from our travels? What is your relationship with that person? When did you last see them?
- I've been having trouble tracking something down. Where have you encountered this item before? What advice do you think I need if I'm trying to obtain it?
- I ask you about a problem you were having the last time you stopped by. Have you made any progress with it?

Browsing, Heading Home

Once all Shoppers have found everything they need, take a moment to look around the market. What do you treat yourself to? What items would be a good gift for another character?

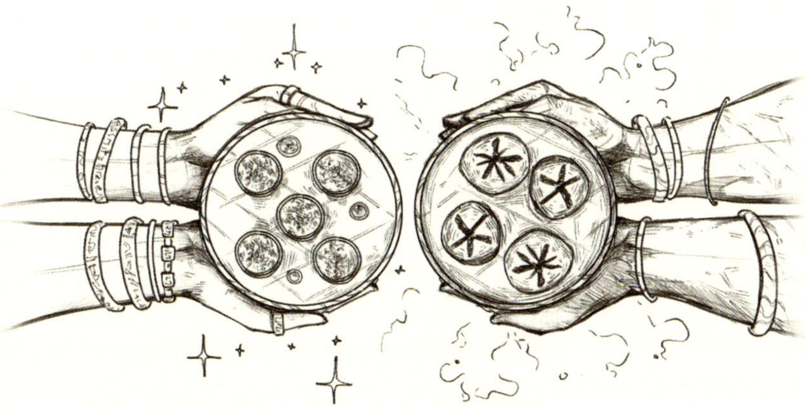

Homegrown

There's something special about using locally grown ingredients. You might have laughed at that before, but you can really notice a difference when you're cooking the same dishes over and over again.

You've got some room for plants and animals, with plenty of magic and food scraps to spare. Why not try it out?

Setup

Anyone can play. As a group, decide where to place your farm. The space can be inside your tavern, but it can also be somewhere relatively close.

You'll also need to decide what you're growing or keeping. Are you doing a little bit of both? What should you start with so you can harvest something soon?

Growing

Farming is messy, gross, and a far cry from the heroics of your adventuring days. As you work, there are quite a few unflattering incidents that occur. But at the end of the day, they're all something you can laugh about together.

Take turns sharing embarrassing stories that happened to your character using any of the prompts. Everyone playing should share at least one.

- There was a... manure accident.
- You found yourself developing a rivalry with a particularly stubborn plant or animal.
- You learned that you have a mild allergy to a plant or animal for the first time.
- One of the baby animals became very fond of you and was affectionate in a rather painful way.
- You ate a plant or mushroom that was by your garden without realizing it wasn't one you grew.
- You chased an animal that ran away and ended up getting lost.
- You were a little too enthusiastic with the magic fertilizer and made some plants way too big.
- You somehow managed to create a new kind of monstrous hybrid plant.
- You got swarmed when you went to feed the animals one day.
- One of your rare plants has a mischievous streak, and it pulled an incredible prank on you.

- Someone played a prank on you and one of the plants or animals became very… unique.
- You kept trying to put clothes on the animals to keep them warm but they kept fighting back.
- You tried to break up a fight between two of the animals but it turned into them ganging up on you instead.
- You had a close call with a mandrake.
- The bee incident.

Harvest

Your hard work pays off. The next time you play ***Wear and Tear***, your Cuisine Rating goes up by one in addition to the upgrade you pick for ***Wear and Tear***. What kind of dishes can you make now that you weren't able to before?

Shelter from the Storm

Early one morning, you feel it. A familiar ache in your bones. Something is coming. As former adventurers, you took extra precautions when you started running the tavern. But there are plenty of people in town that aren't ready. Can you help them in time?

Setup

Someone rushes into the tavern shouting. What calamity is approaching? Choose one.

- A ferocious storm
- A rampaging colossus
- An army of undead
- A curse
- A great flood

Write down the messenger as an NPC. Then, use the prompts to answer individually or as a group:
What precautions did you take in and around the tavern?
What old habits have you struggled to let go of?

- Hiding your valuables in obscure places
- Placing wards that are a mild inconvenience to those around you
- Sleeping with one eye open
- Hidden defenses that spring out of the walls
- A secret signal you still remember
- A divine favor
- Retractable wheels or limbs

Weathering the Storm

Take turns protecting the tavern, the town, or the surrounding area. On your turn, choose an action and ask another adventurer to come with you. This is too big to handle alone.

- Shore up the tavern
- Strategize with the town leaders
- Spread the word to shelter at the tavern
- Cook something to share
- Investigate an old story about the calamity
- Bolster the town's defenses
- Rescue someone stranded
- Head off the calamity, redirect what you can or act as a decoy
- Convince someone stubborn that they need to leave their home
- Spin a story to calm the crowd

Picking Up the Pieces

When the dust has settled, how has the tavern fared? Roll a die.

1-2: Safe. The damage to the tavern is minimal, but parts of the town are totally wrecked. How can you help?

3-4: Damaged. You're not fully operational, but it could have been much worse. You have a lot of repairs ahead of you. Over the next few days, you notice other people in the area swapping their skills and helping each other get back on their feet. What can you offer? Who can you reach out to?

5-6: Wrecked. You made it, but just barely. You stand in the wreckage, trying to understand the extent of the damage. You're going to be closed for a while. Over the next few weeks, which townspeople surprise you by coming to your aid?

A Familiar Face

"Excuse me? Do you know where the tavern is?"

"You're right in front of it! Welcome."

You swear you've seen the stranger's smile before. They lift the hood of their cloak.

"How many years has it been?"

An old friend has come to visit. How do you show them around the town and the tavern?

Setup

Everyone plays. Your friend is someone you all know, but who exactly are they? A member of your party who went their own way? A steady rival? An ally from your most desperate battle?

Draw a map of the town. Mark the tavern's location and any important details from the game so far. You'll add in more locations and details as you play.

Giving the Tour

Each player character shows off a part of the tavern. What would your friend appreciate? What is your favorite part? What are you most proud of? When you're done with the tavern tour, head out into town.

Takes turns introducing a location in town. To get to a location, you must first describe the path you take to get there. If you're not currently introducing a location, you can play as the friend.

Once someone has finished showing off their location, the next player describes their path and location. Once each character has shown off at least one location, move on to ***See You Again*** when you feel ready.

EXAMPLE PATHS

- An alley run by stray cats
- A scenic view
- Slipping through a crowd
- Up a steep hill
- Walking down a street lined with trees
- A magical shortcut
- A short boat ride
- Holding on to a rope
- Jumping a stone wall
- Along the rooftops
- Over a bridge
- Squeezing through a fence

EXAMPLE LOCATIONS

- Somewhere you're a regular
- A majestic tree
- Somewhere that has delicious food
- A hidden gem
- A specialty store
- A quiet corner
- Down by the water
- A show
- A place with an interesting history
- A place where your friends from town hang out
- Somewhere that is special during the current season
- A memorial
- Somewhere magical
- The market stalls

See You Again

Somehow, it's already time for your friend to leave.

How does your group send them off? What are your plans for the next time you see each other?

OPTIONAL: Your friend gives you a Keepsake.

Sliced

You can handle typical tavern food fine. You've got a very nice stew, great bread from a baker down the street, and plenty of ale. But sometimes, supply routes get disrupted. Or maybe you just want to stand out from the rest of the taverns. Whatever the reason, you want to do one thing: cook with monster parts.

Setup

Anyone can play. One player is the COOK. You'll determine the core ingredients of your dish by drawing three cards from a **standard deck of playing cards**. For each card drawn, roll two six-sided dice. Each die determines the size of the monster and its habitat. Then, interpret the card drawn based on its suit and rank.

The rest of the players describe the ingredients in detail and tell you a Highlight of each ingredient or a Difficulty that comes with cooking it. Your character is a competent cook. Just remember to mention how you get around an ingredient's difficulty or you may be criticized for it at the end of the mini-game by the TASTERS.

SIZE

- Tiny
- Small
- Person-sized
- House-sized
- Giant
- Mountain-sized

LOCALE

- Underground
- Snowy region
- Underwater
- Forest
- Desert
- Plains

Ingredient Type

DIAMONDS

Diamonds are seasonings: crushed minerals, rich fermented sauces, powdered spices, flavored oils, thickening agents, etc.

CLUBS

Clubs are fungi, lichens, and molds: fragrant mushrooms, yeasts, bright green and orange slimes, dried lichen, etc.

HEARTS

Hearts are animals and parts of animals: thick juicy steaks, powdered horn, delicate shells, salted tongue, drumsticks, hearts, coarse hair, spit, etc.

SPADES

Spades are plants and plant-based products: fresh berries, dried bark, juice made this morning, starchy roots, crisp leaves, stalks, aromatic flowers, pulp, sweet sap, etc.

FEATURES

A: Magical	**6**: Rare	**10**: Shiny
2: Poisonous	**7**: Natural camouflage	**J**: Parasitic
3: Fragile	**8**: Rancid	**Q**: Ancient
4: Hostile	**9**: Long	**K**: Unique
5: Exoskeleton		

Example Highlights

- If it's cooked appropriately, it is incredibly juicy and tender.
- It has the perfect amount of sweetness, and doesn't overpower the dish.
- It has an interesting texture, and provides variety to the dish.
- It is almost impossible to cook wrong.
- It is easy to add flavor to.
- It pairs very well with a lot of other types of ingredients.
- It's the perfect garnish, adding a lot of complexity.
- You can use it in multiple ways, even in the same dish.

Example Difficulties

- It burns easily if not watched carefully.
- It dries out if overcooked.
- It will look terrible if not prepared properly.
- It is bitter if overcooked.
- It is very easy to overseason.
- It's time-consuming to prepare.
- It's very delicate.
- Eating too much of it gives you that heavy feeling in your gut.

Tasters

The remaining players will play the first people to taste the new dish. It could be a small group of regulars and adventurers or a big tasting event. Each taster has something they want from this dish. Come up with something or use the prompts.

- Something that reminds you of home. Simple, but well-executed.
- A unique combination of flavors.
- A dish that is rich and satisfying, but doesn't leave you feeling bloated afterwards.
- Something refreshing, preferably with lots of fresh fruits or vegetables.
- A new twist on a classic dish. Name and describe the classic dish.
- A dish that really exemplifies the ingredients of the season.
- A spicy dish that still has a good flavor profile.
- Something that includes a trendy new technique or ingredient that you heard about in the next town.
- Mmmm.... Soup.
- Something that's good for eating on the go.

Cooking the Dish

Roll a number of dice equal to four plus your Cuisine Rating. Place the dice on the following chart. Follow the prompts that correspond to the dice results for each category.

GOAL

4-6: *You succeed. A* TASTER *gives you a compliment.*

1-3: *Something goes wrong. The* COOK *describes what happens.*

SEASONING

5-6: *What pleasant memory does the taste of this dish evoke? One* TASTER *answers.*

3-4: *This seems almost right, but it's missing a little something. What flavor do you want more of? Or what spice do you add as you're eating? A* TASTER *answers.*

1-2: *Oh no. What did you forget? Or, what did you put in too much of? The* COOK *answers.*

PRESENTATION

5-6: *Delicately balanced, with the perfect color palette, this dish could be displayed in a museum. A* TASTER *describes a place the dish reminds them of.*

3-4: *The dish looks pretty good. Everything is right where it needs to be. The* COOK *describes one flourish they are proud of.*

1-2: *The dish might taste great, but it looks pretty unappetizing. A* TASTER *describes what part of the dish grosses them out the most.*

TEXTURE

5-6: *A bite that melts in your mouth. The perfect bit of crunch. This dish is a sensory delight. The* COOK *describes what was the most difficult part of achieving the desired texture.*

3-4: *The* COOK *describes how one part of the dish was overcooked or overdone, but you caught it before the dish was ruined.*

1-2: *Food shouldn't be this texture. The* TASTERS *describe what the inedible materials the dish reminds them of.*

Tasting the Dish

After you've finished resolving the prompts, you can write down any new NPCs that liked the dish as regular patrons.

If you make the dish a permanent part of your menu, come up with a name. How do your patrons react to the new dish?

Romancing a Stranger

Someone in the tavern makes eye contact with you and their gaze lingers a little longer than you would expect. Your co-workers urge you on and make every excuse to send you over to talk to the lovely Stranger.

Setup

One pair plays. One player is the ROMANCER, and the other player is the STRANGER.

ROMANCER: Describe a detail about the Stranger that drew you to them.

STRANGER: Describe the first thing you notice about the Romancer.

Getting to Know Each Other

Take turns asking questions, each player should ask two or three.

- I tell a corny joke. Do you laugh, or tell an equally corny joke?
- I name a place you remember visiting. What experience have we shared?
- I compliment you, and you think I'm making fun of you, but I'm completely earnest. What am I complimenting you on?

- I have to step away for a moment, but I look across the room at you. Do our eyes meet, or do you look for me after I look away?
- My hand is close to yours. Do you take it?
- I trip and fall against you. You catch me. What do you say?
- Your past travels have marked you. What am I intrigued by?
- I order my usual and you do the same. What do you say about what I ordered?
- There's music playing and people dancing around us. Will you dance with me? Who asks for the dance?
- You think the food I ordered is weird, but I get you to try some. How do you like it?
- We decide to play a game. Are you terrifyingly good at it? Charmingly terrible?

Closing Time

The tavern is almost empty, and tables are being wiped down. You both get up from the table where you've been talking and wonder where the time has gone.

ROMANCER: Do you say something before the Stranger leaves for the night? Do you go with them? Who is the first person you'll tell about this?

STRANGER: Will you come back to the tavern, tomorrow, or at least some day? Or do you refuse to make a connection, from fear or disinterest? If you decide to return, write down your name on the NPC section of the tavern sheet.

Off the Clock

It's been a while since you've all had a proper day off. Things are slow right now and you can get away with closing up for a day. Where do you go after the tables are wiped down? Who's heard every story you have about the worst people who have walked into the tavern?

Setup

Anyone can play. Each player describes the first thing their character is doing to wind down, let loose, or otherwise forget about work for a while.

Actions

Take turns. On your turn, you can do a scene alone or ask other players to join you. If nothing comes to mind, you can pass, or look at the time and realize you have to get back to work. When everyone has passed in a row, or gone back to work, the mini-game is over.

- Grab some food from around the corner. What's familiar about it?
- Visit a friend. How do you know them and how long has it been since the two of you last met?
- There's a traveling troupe of performers in town for a few days. Have you met any of them before?
- It's the middle of summer, it's scorching hot, and you desperately want to swim. Where's the secret spot you found together?

- Sometimes sparring is the perfect way to blow off steam. What fights do you remember most fondly?
- There's a ball game in the square. Who's the better player?
- It gets a little boring cooking the same things at the tavern almost every day. What experimental dish are you finally going to try?
- It's not that your house is a mess. But it's been a long time since you had the time and energy to do a deep clean from top to bottom. How do you reward yourself when you're done?
- There's a trip you've been wanting to take a little ways from town. You don't usually have enough time, but you do today. Where do you go?
- You sit down and write out a long letter you've been meaning to send. Who are you writing to and what do you tell them?
- There's a spot you found that's perfect for a picnic. Who do you invite and what kinds of foods do you bring?

A Friendly Tavern Brawl

Every tavern has its rowdy patrons. You know they're good at heart, but sometimes when the ale is flowing and spirits are high, things get out of hand. How do you handle the situation?

Setup

Anyone can play. You will need at least two players. Choose between being a Brawler or a De-escalator.

BRAWLERS: What is the disagreement that caused the first punch to be thrown?

DE-ESCALATORS: What made you get involved? Who was the first to intervene?

Breaking Up the Fight

Follow the prompts for each stage of the de-escalation.

APPROACH

De-escalators	Brawlers
You need to interrupt the fight. How do you draw their attention?	*How do you lash out? What do you say that you shouldn't have?*

SEPARATION

De-escalators	Brawlers
How do you keep the brawlers away from each other? Can you get them to focus on something else?	*Try to start the fight back up again.*

TALK-DOWN

De-escalators	Brawlers
How do you ensure that the fight won't break out again tonight?	*As you come down from the fight, what do you feel?*

Setting Things Right

Everyone has been picked up and dusted off. Over the next few days, what do each of your characters do? What happens to the brawlers?

- Get someone home safe
- Repair damage to the tavern
- Help each other recover from your injuries
- Track down an item that was lost in the fray
- Field an apology from a brawler
- Facilitate a reconciliation between the brawlers

Festival Day

Your town is known across the region for its spectacular festivals. How do you prepare? How do you handle the crowds?

Setup

Anyone can play. Play as your adventurer or as a named NPC. What kind of festival is happening today? Each player describes one decoration or feature of the festival. Does your character care about this festival? Do they hate it?

Take turns playing out scenes from the festival. On your turn, ask another player to take on a Challenge from the list, or create one you want to see them attempt. If a player is having trouble thinking of a solution, the group can ask clarifying questions or suggest additional details or complications for the Challenge.

Once you've described how you will resolve a Challenge, flip a coin. On heads, you succeed. On tails, your character is knocked out for the rest of the mini-game.

Each player can use an Experience once during a Challenge to automatically succeed and gain a point. If you're knocked out, you can still attempt Challenges as a named NPC until all of them are knocked out too.

When you've earned five points, or if all characters have been knocked out, whichever happens first, turn to the *Cleaning Up* section.

Challenges

You severely underestimated the amount of prepped ingredients you would need for the festival and have to use a knife faster than you ever have before.	
Heads	*You finish unscathed and gain a point.*
Tails	*You accidentally cut deep into a finger and have to sit out nursing your wound for a while.*

A mishap occurs while sorting luggage and you need to track down several lost bags.	
Heads	*You put the pieces together and track down the bags in no time at all. Gain a point.*
Tails	*You chase dead end after dead end for hours and no one can get in contact with you.*

A very upset guest is causing a commotion. You draw lots and you've gotten the short straw.	
Heads	*You calm them down quickly and manage to compensate them for the trouble. Gain a point.*
Tails	*They talk your ear off and you barely manage to excuse yourself hours later.*

The regulars egg you on to take part in a contest while you're working, and they're very insistent.	
Heads	*You put it away with the best of them to roars of approval and gain a point.*
Tails	*About halfway through you start feeling very sick and need to recuperate out back for a while.*

An adventurer is a little careless in handling a magical artifact and it goes haywire in the middle of the festivities.	
Heads	*It's contained with only a few hats blown off and maybe a table upturned. Gain a point.*
Tails	*You have to shepherd guests out of the room and wrestle with the magical mayhem alone for the rest of the night.*

Supplies are running low, and there's no chance to replace them exactly. You're going to have to try to improvise.	
Heads	*It works beautifully, and your slapdash solution might actually work better than the original. Gain a point.*
Tails	*You can't seem to get it quite right, and you get bogged down trying to make it work for a long time.*

There's a rough storm on its way, but you might be able to board everything up and weather it out if it just grazes you.

Heads	*Your preparations hold. Festival-goers huddle inside as the wind howls, but it's over in half an hour. Gain a point.*
Tails	*The storm is too strong. Everything threatens to break as you run around frantically trying to keep the wind out.*

The equipment you're using for the stand you've set up in the town square isn't exactly new, but it's giving you more trouble than usual.

Heads	*You tie some hasty knots and kick just the right spot and now it all works beautifully. Gain a point.*
Tails	*Nothing you do is working. Orders are taking longer and longer to finish. You're going to be stuck here for a while.*

Business has slowed down because of a competing place nearby and you need to come up with a way to draw more people in fast.	
Heads	*You cause exactly the right kind of commotion and people are crowding through the door again. Gain a point.*
Tails	*Each time you try something new, they try to outdo you. You're bringing in more people again but you can't let up.*

A dancer has gotten injured before the big group dance that's happening right in the center of town. A friend drags you into it as a replacement by calling in a favor.	
Heads	*Your friend is a really good teacher and gives you a few tips in case you forget some steps. The dance goes off without a hitch. Gain a point.*
Tails	*It takes you ages and ages to memorize all the steps. You get it down but you're gone for hours and hours.*

A small child has gotten separated from their parents in the commotion of the festival. They've become rather attached very quickly.	
Heads	*The kid's descriptions aren't the most helpful, but you get lucky and the parents end up coming to the stall and you recognize them instantly. Gain a point.*
Tails	*The kid drags you around the festival, searching for their parents but also convinces you to get them snacks and prizes from the mini-games.*

Cleaning Up

It's finally over. As the festival draws to a close, count up your points. If your characters earned five or more points, you can upgrade the tavern by increasing a Tavern Rating. If all your characters got knocked out, describe how everyone helps each other recover from the chaos.

Finally, take turns coming up with reviews of the festival and your tavern's participation from random townspeople. This could be whispers of conversation overheard around town, a mention in a local newspaper column, or even a social media post depending on your setting.

Good and bad, what did festival attendees have to say about the tavern? What will your characters remember?

Retracing

Adventuring never left you much free time. Starting the tavern was exhausting, but it's the slow season now. You could close up for a while if you wanted. As you talk, you all realize you've left something unresolved from the old days. Maybe it's time for a long journey.

Setup

Everyone plays. Draw a map of the surrounding area. Fill in the tavern's location. You'll add in your route and locations as you play. You can also add details from previous mini-games.

On the Road

Take turns introducing locations by drawing a card and using the prompts to recall your memories of that location.

If you don't like the prompts or struggle to come up with something, discard the card and draw a new one. You can also ask the other players for help.

Once the location and memories are described, players should answer these questions:

- How long has it been since we were last here?
- How has this place changed?

Then, reenact a scene from the past, play out a scene in the present, or move on to the next location.

After each character has introduced at least one location, move on to *Home Again* when you feel ready.

DIAMONDS

Diamonds were beautiful places: A cliff with a breathtaking view, a serene spring, a mountain shrine, the sky castle, a glittering crystal cave, the ancient forest, an abandoned temple with a strange statue, a golden ship, vibrant wetlands, a city by the sea, the edge of the world, the mysterious garden, the painter's house, etc.

CLUBS

Clubs were dangerous places: Battlefields, treacherous ravines, a gnarled forest, a struggling outpost split into two factions, a rocky coast, a wizard's tower, a mountain range covered in deep snow, a city full of corruption, haunted ruins, a weathered ancient ritual site, twisting tunnels, a tempting illusion, a royal court, etc.

HEARTS

Hearts were joyful places: A castle where you were rewarded, a mountain village in spring, the city that held a massive feast, a town during a harvest festival, the packed outdoor theater, the town where you lifted a curse, the tavern where you celebrated after defeating a dragon, the old tournament grounds, etc.

SPADES

Spades were restful places: A forest clearing where you camped, a witch's house, a dry cave in a storm, a quiet but welcoming inn, a beach under starlight, a farm in the middle of nowhere, a warm castle in winter, inside a giant hollow tree, a secret base, a train with great food and plenty of room, the perfect city park, etc.

A. We used to pass through here often in our travels.

2. We couldn't handle the curse that was here.

3. We had a certain reputation here.

4. Someone we knew died here.

5. Someone helped us out a great deal here.

6. We got into an argument here.

7. We borrowed something from this place.

8. We took on an unusual request here.

9. This place haunted us for a while.

10. We left something here.

J. We met a good friend here.

Q. We ate something incredibly delicious here.

K. We stayed for a while and got used to living here.

Home Again

Return to the tavern. Each character chooses a prompt.

- You notice something about the tavern you could only notice after a long time away.
- You notice how something has changed in the time you've been gone.
- You notice how someone in your group has changed after the journey.
- You brought something back from a location. What do you do with it?
- You plan to return to a location again sometime in the future.

A Bard's Tale

During your time as an adventurer, you accomplished many daring deeds. In fact, some of those deeds are retold to this day by traveling bards.

Setup

One pair plays. One player is the BARD, and the other player is the ADVENTURER. The Adventurer should be a player character or a named NPC. The Bard may be a player character or any NPC. To start, answer the questions for each role.

ADVENTURER: What detail of the story makes you realize that this tale or song is about you?

BARD: How did you learn this tale? Is it directly from the mouth of an eyewitness? Another bard? Did you piece together the story from multiple versions?

Each player takes turns recounting the tale. The Bard uses prompts from ***Telling the Tale***. The Adventurer uses prompts from ***Interruptions***. Each player should take two or three turns depending on the story.

Telling the Tale

- What is the most popular part of the story that everyone agrees upon? Adventurer, is this part actually correct?
- What dramatic flourish have you added to please the audience?
- How long ago did the events of the tale take place? Adventurer, when did they actually take place?
- What part of the story is a guaranteed tearjerker?
- Your memory of this part of the story is a little hazy and you're stumbling through it. What noise or sign from the Adventurer makes you tell it with a little more conviction?
- What part of the story were you drawn to in the first place? What part is your favorite?
- What detail of the story seems outrageous, even to you? Do you sell it convincingly or can the audience tell your heart's not in it? Adventurer, is it true?
- Do you know any other stories about this adventurer? Do you mention any of them?
- What part of storytelling do you think is most important? How does that show in the way you tell this tale?
- What mistake do you make while telling the story? Can you make it work without the audience catching on?
- Why did you choose to tell this story tonight?

Interruptions

- What part of the story do you forcibly take over because you would hate to hear it told wrong?
- What part of the story do you find yourself telling unconsciously, word for word in sync with the bard?
- What part of this tale is your least favorite? Why?
- It's impossible to capture this part of the story in words. What makes you nudge the person next to you and say to them, "You had to be there."
- What chance do you take to spin the tall tale even taller?
- Why is your head in your hands? Why is this part of the story embarrassing?
- What part of this retelling almost makes you tackle the bard off the stage? Why is it infuriating?
- What part of this story can you see in your head, as clear as the day it happened?
- Who's the real villain of the story?
- What scar or mark on you aches as you hear this story?

Ending the Tale

When the tale has come to a close, answer the following questions.

BARD: What is the epilogue of the tale? Does it have a moral to convey? Are you being cheered or heckled?

ADVENTURER: What happened after the tale that no one else could have known? Are you happy with how the story was told?

A Glass of the Gods

Adventurers love to wind down after a long journey with a drink. Most of the time they just have several rounds of whatever's cheap and cause a harmless ruckus. But sometimes a troubled adventurer comes in looking for answers at the bottom of a glass.

Maybe you faced the same trouble before. Maybe you're just a shoulder to lean on. In any case, you feel a responsibility to ask the right questions and make the perfect drink, something that can help the adventurer look inside and find an answer or a path forward.

Setup

One pair plays. One player is the ADVENTURER, and the other player is the BARTENDER. The Adventurer can be a player character, a regular, or a new face. The Bartender should be a player character or a named NPC.

ADVENTURER: Decide whether you'd like an alcoholic drink or a non-alcoholic drink. Next, figure out what's troubling you. Come up with something on your own, or use one of the prompts.

- A lover has grown distant while you were away adventuring.
- A member of your party died while out in the wild or down in the dungeon, and you miss them dearly.
- Your party never seems to find enough treasure, and fights over money are always breaking out.
- You were badly injured on your last adventure and you have doubts that you can continue being an adventurer.
- Your deity asks so much of you, and you question if your faith is really worth it.
- Although you love adventuring, recently you've been missing home. Or, you don't feel like you have a home to return to.
- Violence is part of the job, but you can't shake the feeling that you have innocent blood on your hands.

BARTENDER: Describe the current atmosphere of the tavern and one detail about the adventurer that draws your attention.

Mixing the Glass

The Bartender asks questions, and the Adventurer answers. Ask as many as necessary.

- How strong do you like your drinks?
- What reminds you of home?
- Do you have a sweet tooth?
- Where was your last adventure?
- Is there a taste that you hate?
- Why did you become an adventurer?
- What are the tenets of your faith?
- Are you sleeping well at night?
- Do you have a favorite fruit?
- What is the most beautiful thing you've seen on an adventure?
- What is the most terrifying thing you've seen on an adventure?
- Who or what was the toughest foe you've defeated?
- Who or what was the toughest foe you couldn't defeat?

A Glass of the Gods

Presenting and Drinking the Glass

Once there are no more questions to ask, the Bartender mixes the drink. It could be a specialty cocktail, a wine or spirit hidden deep in the cellar, an herbal tea, or a spiced cider. Finally, each player resolves their final prompts.

BARTENDER: Create a drink for the Adventurer to soothe their troubles. Is there a story to this drink? Where is it from? Who was it first made for?

ADVENTURER: Have you gained a new perspective on your problems after this? Can you move forward? Can you let go?

If you're having trouble coming up with a drink, put something together using these example components.

BASE DRINK	SYRUPS AND FLAVORS	GRANISHES
Shaken cocktail	*Lavender*	*Orange peel*
Frozen drink	*Angostura bitters*	*Salt rim*
Coffee	*Lime juice*	*Cinnamon stick*
Hot chocolate	*Grapefruit juice*	*Preserved cherry*
Broth	*Ginger*	*Fresh herbs*
Apple cider	*Hot sauce*	*Egg foam*
Tea	*Elderflower syrup*	*Cocoa powder*
Sparkling water	*Peppermint*	*Tapioca pearls*
Tomato juice	*Blackberry*	*Cayenne pepper*
Wine	*Mulling spices*	*Rose petals*
Yogurt	*Hibiscus*	*Rock candy*

A Distinguished Guest

Someone important is in town, and they're almost here. The tavern has to be at its best for this guest. After all, they might leave a generous tip.

Setup

Anyone can play. As a group, figure out a few details about the important guest. Where do they come from? How important are they? Have you heard of them before?

One player plays the GUEST. The other players take on the Challenges. Each Challenge tests one of your Tavern Ratings.

Cuisine Challenge

Describe your preparations for this special meal. You'll probably need several courses and something that highlights local products.

In order to pass the challenge, flip a coin. You get a number of attempts equal to your Cuisine Rating. If any Challenger has an Experience that they used in the scene, you get an additional attempt.

HEADS: You pass. The Guest describes what they most enjoy about the meal.

TAILS: If all coin flips are tails, you fail. The Guest describes something unpleasant they find in their food.

Atmosphere Challenge

Describe what you do to make the tavern look and feel welcoming. Are there special decorations? Do you hire local musicians?

In order to pass the challenge, flip a coin. You get a number of attempts equal to your Atmosphere Rating. If any Challenger has an Experience that they used in the scene, you get an additional attempt.

HEADS: You pass. The Guest describes a special memory they will always have of their stay.

TAILS: If all coins are tails, you fail. The Guest describes something in the tavern that is considered passé in their culture.

Service Challenge

Describe how you organize the NPCs so that everything goes smoothly. Who is in charge of what?

In order to pass the challenge, flip a coin. You get a number of attempts equal to your Service Rating. If any Challenger has an Experience that they used in the scene, you get an additional attempt.

HEADS: You pass. The Guest describes an interesting conversation they have with someone at the tavern.

TAILS: If all coins are tails, you fail. The Guest describes a frustration they have with the service at the tavern.

A Lavish Gift

If you pass two or more Challenges, you succeed in impressing your Guest. The Guest describes a lavish gift and presents it to the Tavern before they leave. This gift helps you instantly upgrade one of your TAVERN RATINGS.

A Funeral

It feels like just yesterday you were sitting together around a fire, tired from a long day of traveling but happy to be in good company.

As an adventurer, you've said farewell many times. Sometimes it was only temporary. Most of the time, it wasn't.

Setup

Everyone plays. The person who passed away was someone you all knew well, but who were they exactly? Was it one of you? Another member of your party? An old friend? A townsperson?

When you have decided, move on to *In Loving Memory*.

In Loving Memory

These questions represent how everyone talks about and remembers your departed friend. They can be asked during a funeral or similar ceremony. Alternatively, they can come up in the weeks, months, or years after your friend has passed.

Take turns asking each other questions. After each character has answered at least one question, move on to ***Last Moments*** when you feel ready to.

EXAMPLE QUESTIONS

- How did you meet? How did you become friends?
- What kind of person were they?
- When was the last time you saw them?
- How did they want to be laid to rest?
- How did they want to be remembered?
- What is your favorite memory of them? When did they get on your nerves?
- What were they an expert in? What did they refuse to learn?
- What was their favorite food?
- What did you love about them?
- What did they love? What did they hate?
- How did most people see them? How did you see them?
- What did they love to complain about?
- What topic could they talk endlessly about?
- What were they proud of?
- What's something they did that made you proud?
- What ritual or habit reminds you of them? What part of them has stuck with you?
- What Keepsake did they give you?
- Who have they left behind? What communities were they a part of?

Last Moments

Flip a coin to determine your group's final scene:

HEADS: A flashback of your group at your friend's side during their final moments.

TAILS: A flashback of when you heard the news about the sudden death of your friend.

In the Rhythm of Things

Time passes. Rough edges are sanded down. Before you know it, life in town has become like breathing. You gather in your favorite part of the tavern and wonder where the time has gone.

Setup

This is the last game. Everyone plays. Everyone takes turns describing a habit their character picked up while living here. Then, proceed to the ending questions.

Ending Questions

Everyone takes turns asking each other questions. The game is over when everyone has answered two questions.

- What was the hardest part of fitting into town?
- Who helped you the most as you acclimated?
- What is your favorite memory of your time here?
- What surprised you the most about living in town?
- What was the best dish you remember eating that one of you made?
- What was the worst dish you remember eating that one of you made?
- Where is your favorite place in town?
- What do you miss about adventuring?

- What do you not miss about adventuring?
- With the tavern running smoothly, what do you want to spend more time doing, for yourself?
- What touch have you added to make the place you live feel like home?
- If you got sick, who would come care for you?
- What's something you can't believe you lived without back when you were adventuring?
- Do you have any plans to travel soon?
- What are you most proud of yourself for?
- Where have you put your Keepsakes?
- Who's coming over for dinner tomorrow?
- Where do you go when you need to think or calm down?
- What tradition do you now share with someone?
- What's a neat trick you've learned?
- What do you look forward to every week?

Recipes

DRAGON HOTPOT

For the broth:
1 dragon's tear
2 segments of sea serpent spine

For sauce:
Any fermented salty sauce
Wine or vinegar
Sugar
Minced mana root

Hotpot ingredients:
3 mandrakes (leaves and bodies separated, chopped into bite-size pieces)
1 burdock root (shaved into strips)
1 bunch of medicinal herbs
Thinly sliced dragon meat (can substitute slices of walking mushroom)
Freshly picked mushrooms
A handful of dried slime noodles
A spoonful of cooking oil

To make the broth, simmer the bones in the tear for an hour. Mix desired sauce ingredients to taste. Add a little to the pot and sear off some of the meat before filling the pot with broth and ingredients. Top off with more sauce, broth, and ingredients as the pot gets low.
Optional: Dip ingredients in raw basilisk egg to add creaminess and to mellow out the salty sweet flavor of the sauce.

Cook At Home Recipes

Due to the success of the crowdfunding campaign that brought Stewpot to market, we've been able to commission four fantasy themed recipes you can actually cook in your home. These dishes were crafted by food author Krista D. Ball to bring you comfort and warm your soul in the same cozy spirit of the game. They include traditional and vegetarian options and should be easy to prepare without sophisticated cooking skills or a fancy kitchen. Whether you make them yourself or for your friends to share around an evening exploring Stewpot, we hope you enjoy the warmth, creativity, and goodwill which went into creating them.

My autobiography could be written as a recipe book.

From my upbringing in Newfoundland, Canada, where I ate foods like molasses on fried bread dough, Jig's Dinner, and scrunchions, and where it was perfectly normal to buy lobster from the back of a guy's truck. To the happy moments, such as my 2018 trip to Lerwick where I ate these otherworldly cheese parcels. The scary times. The sad times. Food was always there. And, the times it was not? Its very absence was something to note.

These four recipes are all designed to bring you comfort. To warm your soul. To help you experiment. To make mistakes and laugh. I want you to write your own autobiography in my childhood molasses cookies.

- Krista D. Ball,
creator of the following recipes

1

Dwarven Lassy Drops

The only thing the Stormhand brothers ever agreed upon was their mother's molasses cookies. Of course, Duwant was never satisfied with something Dewent liked and eventually published his version of the recipe, much to his brother's annoyance. Regardless of which version is best, innkeepers still bake these cookies whenever important guests visit to chase away foul smells.

—EXCERPT FROM "BROTHERS TO RIVALS: THE UNAUTHORIZED BIOGRAPHY OF DWARVEN MERCENARIES DEWENT AND DUWANT STORMHAND"

Dwarven Lassy Drops

(vegetarian)

Yield: 2-3 dozen cookies

- ½ cup (125mL) fancy molasses
- 1 cup (200g) brown sugar, packed
- ¾ cup (170g) room temperature butter
- 1 large egg
- 3 cups (400g) all-purpose flour
- 1 tsp cinnamon
- 1 tsp ground ginger
- ¼ tsp ground cloves
- 1 tsp baking soda

Preheat the oven to 350°F/175°C. Line a baking sheet with parchment paper. Cream the molasses, brown sugar, and butter together. Once the mixture is smooth and glossy, gently whisk the egg with a fork, then fold into the mixture.

Spoon flour into measuring cups if not weighing. Combine the flour, spices, and baking soda in a separate bowl. Slowly incorporate the dry ingredients into the egg-butter mixture until thoroughly mixed. If the mixture is too wet, add a little extra flour (a tablespoon at a time) until you can shape it into walnut-sized balls.

Place the balls on a lined baking sheet. Use your fingers to slightly flatten the tops of the balls. Bake for 10 minutes. Remove from oven and let cool on the baking sheet for 5 minutes. Place cookies on wire racks to cool completely.

Duwant's Version: Replace the cinnamon with cardamom. Roll the balls in granulated sugar and then press down with a fork.

Dad's Version: Add ½ cup (60g) of walnuts, then cover the cooled cookies with icing when Mom isn't looking.

2

Grass Pie

We were understandably nervous that day. The eastern orcs had sent their first envoys to the elven lands in four decades. The kitchen was in a panic. No one knew what East Coast orcs even ate at that point! The Prime Minister approved my menu ahead of time, which included her favorite dish—spinach pie. However, when the pie was presented to Frak, the seniormost orc, he pounded his fist upon the table and shouted, "You dare serve us grass!"

Then, into the stunned silence, Frak shouted (but with a grin this time), "We eat spinach pie, too!" The room erupted in relieved laughter.

And, so, that is why we eat "grass" pie on Treaty Day.

FROM THE THREE LILIES, THE OFFICIAL COOKBOOK OF THE ELVEN PRIME MINISTER'S PERSONAL CHEF, RETIRED.

Grass Pie

(vegetarian)

Servings: 6 servings

- 1 onion, finely chopped
- 4 cloves garlic, minced
- Oil of choice for frying
- 1lb (454g) frozen spinach, thawed and drained
- 3/4 cup (200g) ricotta cheese, drained
- 1/3 cup (30g) grated parmesan cheese
- 1 tsp salt
- ½ tsp each of dried dill, dried oregano, and red pepper flakes
- 3 tbsp pesto (basil or tomato…or both)
- 2 eggs, beaten
- 1 egg, beaten with a splash of milk (for the crust)
- Prepared pie crust dough

Fry the onion and garlic with a little oil on low heat until fragrant and translucent but not browned.

Let the onion mixture cool slightly before mixing them with the cheeses, spices, pesto, and two beaten eggs. Give the spinach a final squeeze to ensure all the liquid is out, then add to the mixture.

Line a pie pan (or several small tart pans) with the pie crust, ensuring it goes over the sides of the pan. Add the spinach filling. Add a second sheet of pie dough on top, or cut out decorative shapes and carefully lay on top. Cut off any remaining dough about the edge. Brush the top with the eggy milk. Add a few slits if using a full top crust.

Bake in a 375°F/190°C oven for 45–55 minutes or until the crust is golden brown. Let the pie rest for at least 10 minutes before cutting.

Pies the Limit: *You can use any refrigerator pie dough or your favorite apple pie crust dough. If you use frozen puff pastry, just follow the box's instructions.*

Game of Chicken: *Add a handful of leftover cooked, chopped chicken breast.*

3

Nan's Gruel

Nan's Gruel is the perfect remedy for cold, damp mornings. With no standard recipe beyond personal tastes, countless versions of this hearty traveler's breakfast are found in all decent taverns across the High Mountains. Part of the charm of Nan's Gruel is that you can use almost any grain (adjusting water and cooking times). Caution: don't use quick-cook or instant grains, as that is how you make glue.

—EXCERPT FROM FOOD FROM HIGH, A FOOD-LOVER'S GUIDE TO THE HIGH MOUNTAINS.

Nan's Gruel

(vegetarian)

Servings: 6 servings

- 1 cup (255g) pearl barley
- 3 cups (750mL) broth or water
- 4 shallots, finely chopped
- 4 cloves garlic, finely chopped
- Salt and hot sauce (Sriracha, Gochujang, etc.), adjusted to taste

Bring the water to a boil in a pot and add the barley, salt, and hot sauce. Stir well and cover. You can also use a rice cooker.

Turn the heat to low and simmer for about thirty minutes or until the barley is cooked. If using a pot, check occasionally to see if more water is needed to prevent sticking. Take off heat and let stand for 5–10 minutes covered to soak up any additional water.

While the barley is cooking, fry the shallots and garlic in a little oil or butter on low heat until the shallots are translucent but not browned. Add the mixture to the cooked barley. The gruel can be eaten as is or as one of the variations below.

Daily Special Variations

I've Barley Seen You Lately: Cook as above, then add 2 tbsp chopped pecans, ½ chopped avocado, 1 tsp nutritional yeast or parmesan cheese, and a dash of red pepper flakes to each serving. Stir well.

Winter Defense: Cook as above, then add a cooked potato, 2 pieces of cooked bacon, 1 soft boiled egg, and top with ½ oz shredded cheddar, a chopped green onion, and extra hot sauce to each serving.

Warm and Cozy: Replace some (or all) of the liquid with milk (or a milk alternative) and add 1 tsp salt. Leave out the other ingredients. Cook as above, but watch carefully; this can burn easily! When serving, add a handful of berries, some sliced almonds, a sprinkle each of cinnamon and nutmeg, and a drizzle of honey.

4

Pinky's Definitely Not Pink Soup (with Doughballs)

Our cook ran off with a local fire demon girl two hours before our ship left the dock. Despite having never boiled a pot of water in my life, I was promoted to head cook. I was keen to make a good impression and set about making our crew's favorite dish: split pea soup.

My first batch was pitched overboard, and the captain threatened to throw me overboard with the second batch. The third, though? That was when I learned purple carrots turn food bright pink.

Thus, the name stuck until this very day.

AN EXCERPT FROM PINKY THE COOK'S "SAILS AND SOUP: AN ORC ON THE NINE SEAS."

Pinky's Definitely Not Pink Soup

(with Doughballs)

Servings: 6–8 servings

Soup

- 7oz (200g) bacon, chopped
- 2 onions, finely chopped
- 2 stalks of celery, diced small
- 10 cups (2.5L) water or broth
- 2 cups (450g) dried yellow or green split peas (450g), rinsed
- 2 carrots, diced small
- 1 small turnip/ rutabaga/swede, diced small
- 2 bay leaves
- Thyme
- Rosemary, a few sprigs
- 1 tsp pepper

Doughballs

- 1 1/4 cups (150g) all-purpose flour
- 1 tsp baking powder
- 2 tbsp (30g) cold butter
- 1/3–1/2 cup (80–120 mL) cold water

In a soup pot, fry the onions, celery, and bacon together over low heat (about 15-20 minutes) until cooked but not browned. Drain off excess grease. Add 10 cups (2.5L) water to the cooked onions and bring to a boil. Add the peas and turn the heat to low, with the pot loosely covered. Cook for 30 minutes.

Add the chopped vegetables to the soup and taste the soup broth to see if it needs more salt (or anything else to your taste). Cook loosely covered for 15 minutes.

While the vegetables are cooking, make your doughballs. Using just your fingertips or a pastry knife, mix the butter into the flour and baking powder until crumbly. Slowly add the water until a lumpy ball forms. Don't overmix. Cut into 8 pieces and roll into balls.

Drop the balls on top of the soup and cook for 15 minutes. Keep the pot covered tightly.

Serve with one or two of the doughballs.

Pixie's Choice: (Vegetarian) Replace the bacon with oil to fry the onions. Adjust the salt. Adding a dash or two of liquid smoke would not be amiss either.

Bacon Lover's Quest: Try this with different types of bacon or smoked pork. Depending on the leanness of the meat, you might need to add or drain the fat.

Sailor's Delight: Adventurous tavern owners who wish to recreate the soup of port cities can replace the bacon with 100g of salt pork. Or, add chopped salt beef (such as cured navel beef) to the soup for a surprising addition. Presoak the beef and cook according to the packaging before adding it to the soup, or it'll be inedible.

DANIEL HERNANDEZ ✦ *Artist* ✦ *she/her*

Hello everyone! I'm more known as Xylica and I enjoy drawing sapphic experiences mostly for my personal work! For my commissions and projects, i absolutely enjoy drawing couples and fantasy themed illustrations! As a game of thrones nerd, being part of these kind of projects makes me really happy! I hope everyone will get to enjoy our work for this project.

LINDEN MEDINA ✦ *Artist* ✦ *he/him*

Linden is an LA based illustrator and comic artist who enjoys cafe hopping with friends. He also enjoys his share of both slice of life romance and horror/thriller manga!

FRANZ MICHAEL A. BAUTISTA ✦ *Artist* ✦ *he/him*

A creative artist based in SEA. I draw and paint pieces ranging from character illustrations, concept art, and design!

RHIE CUEVA ✦ *Artist* ✦ *she/they*

Rhie is a PH-based artist doing illustration on the side as they fight their through university. They love stories, storytelling, and being able to merge that with visual art.

KELSEY PHILLIPS ✦ *Artist*

Hello, I'm Kelsey (aka "keymintt"), an Arizona-based illustrator and comic artist who specializes in monsters, people, and everything in-between. If I'm not drawing, I'm often teaching k-12 students how to draw dragons, anime characters, and desert wildlife.

LORNE COLT ✦ *Artist* ✦ *he/they*

Lorne Colt is a nerd with a voracious appetite for information and a distinct love of character acting, world building, and random generators. They've worked for more than a decade as a general artist and animator, largely for rad indie projects and creators.

ELEMEI ✦ *Artist*

Grown in the US Southeast, Elemei likes drawing and dislikes being cold.

ODDESQUE ✦ *Artist* ✦ *they/them*

Illustrator based in India. Enjoys listening to ambient music and drawing mechs.

ARTHUR CABEZAS ✦ *Artist* ✦ *he/they*

Arthur is a Filipino illustrator and comic artist who tells stories about furious trans kids with the gods and animals from his backyard. He has illustrated for projects with Evil Hat, Darrington Press, Gubat Banwa, and Sina Una.

JASPRISMATIC ✦ *Artist* ✦ *he/him*

As vibrant as the tropical paradise of the Philippines and a heart as warm as the Filipino sun, Jasper's illustrations reflect his deep connection to the vastness of nature and his fascination towards animals around the world. The twenty-seven year old digital illustrator resides within the provincial towns of Polomolok, South Cotabato. Drawing inspiration from diverse sources during his childhood, Jasper's creation evokes a sense of wonder & curiosity that continues to push the boundaries of his creativity.

NPCS

NAME:

PRONOUNS:

NAME:

PRONOUNS:

NAME:

PRONOUNS:

NAME:

PRONOUNS:

NAME:

PRONOUNS:

NAME:

PRONOUNS:

TAVERN SHEET

NAME

LOCATION

LOOK

stewpot

TAVERN RATINGS

CUISINE

◆ *A cramped kitchen. Plenty of staples but nothing fancy.* **1**

◇ *A modest kitchen. New friends at the market.* **2**

◇ *A bustling kitchen. Brand new cookware. A well-stocked spice cabinet.* **3**

◇ *A splendid kitchen. Good deals on ingredients and fresh deliveries. Specialized tools.* **4**

ATMOSPHERE

◆ *Comfortable enough, but a little boring. Things feel slightly off.* **1**

◇ *A little plain, but homey. Not a bad place to get a good night's sleep.* **2**

◇ *Furniture and decorations that highlight the area. Lots of personal touches. It's really starting to come together.* **3**

◇ *The comfiest beds you've ever slept in. Lots of light and good company. Adventurers seek you out after long journeys.* **4**

SERVICE

◆ *A former farmhand, an injured local guard.* **1**

◇ *An experienced line cook, good wait staff.* **2**

◇ *An interior decorator, a skilled executive chef.* **3**

◇ *An accomplished head of staff, a prestigious sommelier.* **4**

ADVANCEMENT DETAILS

Each time a Tavern Rating increases, each player may describe a new detail or feature for the tavern.

CHARACTER SHEET

NAME: ______________________ ________
pronouns

LOOK: ______________________

WEAPON	
ARMOR	
QUIRK	

ADVENTURER JOB	ADVENTURER EXPERIENCES

TOWN JOB	TOWN EXPERIENCES

Keepsakes

stewpot